BOOKS  THE BIG GOD B

BIG GOD BOOKS  THE BIG GOD BOOKS

 THE BIG GOD BOOKS  THE BIG GO

BOOKS  THE BIG GOD BOOKS  THE

BIG GOD BOOKS  THE BIG GOD BOOKS

 THE BIG GOD BOOKS  THE BIG GO

BOOKS THE BIG GOD BOOKS THE

BIG GOD BOOKS THE BIG GOD BOOKS

 THE BIG GOD BOOKS THE BIG GO

BOOKS  THE BIG GOD BOOKS  THE BIG GOD

# THE BIG GOD BOOKS
# A LITTLE LUNCH

Written by **Gabe Olson** and **Andrea Olson**
Art by **Elisa Patrissi**

For **Sophia, Adeley** and **Ayla**

We pray that these books give you
a tangible reminder that God is always working,
always for you, even if things turn out differently
than you thought they would.
May you remember there are countless miracles
happening around you every day.
And never forget to live in gratitude for them.
We love you and can't wait to continue witnessing
miracles together.
Love,
Dad and Mom

ISBN 978-1-7374374-1-3 (Hardcover Edition)
Art by Elisa Patrissi • Design by Josh Beatman/Brainchild Studios
First printing September 2021. Printed in the United States of America.
Published by Something New Publishing
somethingnewpublishing.com

Hi! I'm G!
Want to hear a little story about my big God?
Come inside and see!

That's my mom. She helps people.
She puts bandages on boo-boos.
She gives people food.
She teaches people about God's love.
She helps people—like me!—every day!

One time, she planned a big party.
It took many days to get ready.
She worked on the party all day and at night.
She found many helpers.
She made invitations.
She picked out a LOT of music.

This party would help lots of people
hear what is true about God.
With singing and laughing and learning
and a little lunch for everyone!

So we invited many, many people!
Loud and tall or shy and small,
friends and neighbors and
family members.
We asked God to fill every seat in the great big room.
Because there's nothing our big God can't do!

The people making the lunches asked my mom,
"How many people will come?"
Hmm. My mom wondered.
If every seat was filled,
we would need many, many lunches!

But what if people didn't come to the party?
If we ordered many lunches,
there might be lots and LOTS of leftovers!

Mom wanted to make a wise choice.
She asked God to help her.
She said, "There's nothing our big God can't do!"
So she ordered many, many lunches!

On the day of the party, we all had great fun!
There was singing and laughing and learning
and a little lunch for everyone!
But how many people came to the party?
Was every seat filled?
What do you see?

No! Every seat was NOT filled.
Only a few people came.
Many, many seats were empty.
Many, many lunches were not eaten.
What happened?
We wanted to help so many people.
Didn't God hear our prayers?

Suddenly, a man walked into the party room.
He was looking for LUNCH!
But not just one little lunch.
This man needed many, many lunches
to help many, many hungry people.
But he didn't have enough money to buy them.
He came to ask for help.

My mom heard the man's problem.
She was filled with joy!
She ran up to the man to tell him
about all the leftover lunches!
We gave them away.
The man was so happy!
And guess what?
We helped so many people!

Every seat was not filled.
But every hungry stomach was filled that day.
God DID hear our prayers!
And God heard the man's prayers too!
Mom prayed for help and bought many, many lunches.
God used them to help many, many people.
There's nothing our big God can't do!

## Start the conversation

Miracles are gifts from God. Sometimes they are the big things that we ask for. Other times, they are gifts that we didn't ask for but are exactly what we need. This story about the little lunches is true! We were there. The thing this story taught us is that sometimes God works in big ways and sometimes He works in little ways— but He's always working for our good! The Big God Books were created to help children see the ways God works through everyday miracles.

## Questions to ask

What did God do to help the people in this story? What has God done for you?

## Prayer to pray

Thank you, God, for helping us in big and little ways. When I eat my little lunch, I'll remember to say thank you to my **BIG** God— there's nothing He can't do! Amen.